W9-AHK-883

This book belongs to

....

This is the story of the Runaway Son.

Try reading it yourself – it's a lot of fun!

There's something else. Can you guess what?

On every page there's a hat to spot.

Text copyright © 2006 Nick and Claire Page

This edition copyright © 2006 make believe ideas ltd.

27 Castle Street, Berkhamsted, Herts, HP4 2DW. All rights reserved.

No part of this publication may be reproduced, stored in a retrieval system or

transmitted in any form or by any means, electronic, mechanical, photocopying,

recording, or otherwise, without the prior written permission of the copyright owner.

Manufactured in China.

The Runaway Son

Nick and Claire Page

Illustrations by Sara Baker

make
believe
ideas

Once there was a father –
Farmer Godfrey was his name.
He had two very different sons,
but loved them both the same.
Steady Eddie was the eldest –
he worked hard for his dad.
His younger brother didn't –
they called him **Cheeky Chad**.

Cheeky Chad decided that
he'd like to leave the farm.
He took his father for a walk
and used his **cheeky** charm.
"You know the money, Daddy,
you will leave me when you're dead?
I want to do some traveling,
so I'd like it now instead."

His dad was sad that **Cheeky Chad**
wanted to leave so soon.
And even though he thought his son
was a silly great baboon,
he gave him lots of money
and a wallet to put it in.
And this is how the sassy boy's
adventure did begin.

Chad bought a car, a flashy suit
and headed for the sun.
Every day he partied,
buying drinks for everyone.

The money went, his friends went too,
he had to find a job.
But no one wanted **Cheeky Chad** –
that crazy, lazy slob!

Meanwhile, **Steady Eddie's** work
was slowly plodding on,
while **Farmer Godfrey** wondered
where his younger son had gone.

While farmhands – Terry, Gerry, Perry,
Kerry-Sue and Pete –
were feasting on three meals a day,
with more than they could eat!

Poor and tired and hungry,
Chad bumped into Mrs Briggs,
who offered him some work to do –
looking after pigs!
He thanked her very much –
the boy could not believe his luck,
until he saw he'd spend each day
clearing out the muck.

Poor and tired and hungry,
Chad was dreaming he could fill
his empty, rumbling tummy
with the peelings and pig swill.
Then he remembered how, at home,
the farmhands would all meet,
feasting on three meals a day,
with more than they could eat.

So **Cheeky Chad** made up his mind
to go home to his dad.
"I'll say to him, 'I'm sorry,
I've been wasteful, I've been bad.
I've done you wrong, my Father,
and, God knows, it makes me sad.
Please forgive me, my dear Daddy,
your baddy laddy, **Chad**.'"

He hitched a ride inside a garbage man's
dirty, stinking van.
But as he got to **Godfrey's** farm
he saw a worried man,
leaning on a gate and
looking for his youngest son.
Then **Godfrey** saw his young son's face,
and he began to run!

Hugging one another,
Cheeky Chad apologized.
"It doesn't matter, son," said Dad.
"Just wipe your crying eyes.
Farmhands! Perry, Gerry, Terry,
Pete and Kerry-Sue!
Kill the cow, and do it now,
let's have a barbecue!"

Meanwhile, **Steady Eddie**
kept on digging in the field.
"What's all this?" he asked the crew,
who happily revealed
the plans for a huge party,
with dancing, food, and fun.
Cheeky Chad had come back home –
the party had begun!

Steady Ed rolled up his sleeves,
set off to see his dad.
"I'll say to him, 'It's just not fair,
it really makes me mad.
You've done me wrong, my Father,
and, God knows, it makes me sad,
to see you treating **Chad** like this,
your boy who has been bad.'"

As they approached each other,
Steady Ed fell on one knee.
He grabbed his father's hand and said,
"You never notice me.
He's always been your favorite son,
no matter if it showed,
I may be **Steady Eddie**,
but I'm ready to explode!"

"Ssh," said his dad while hugging **Ed**,
"You've always been around.
We thought that **Chad** was lost,
but now we find that he is found.
Today is great! Let's celebrate!
And now, get on your bike.
I'd do the same for you
because I love you both alike."

"Come, **Steady Ed**, let's celebrate,
my boy, now give me five!
We thought that **Chad** was dead
but now we know that he's alive!'
Come Gerry, Perry!
Come here Terry, Kerry-Sue and Pete!
We'll feast on one huge meal today
with more than we can eat!"

Ready to tell

Oh no! Some of the pictures from this story have been mixed up! Can you retell the story and point to each picture in the correct order?

Picture dictionary

Encourage your child to read these harder
words from the story and gradually develop
their basic vocabulary.

farmhands   father   gate

meal   money   pigs

sons   suit   van

Key words

Here are some key words used in context. Help your child to use other words from the border in simple sentences.

"I **am** going away," said the son.

This is his new car.

He cared **for** pigs.

"I shall **go** home," he said.

He gave him a **big** hug.

Make some wooden spoon puppets

If you'd like to act out this story, why not make puppets of Eddie, Chad and Farmer Godfrey? (You can make characters for other stories or plays in the same way.)

You will need

3 wooden spoons • acrylic or poster paints • paintbrushes • plate or saucer • scissors • string, wool, straw, ribbon • strong glue

What to do

1 Paint both sides of the "bowl" of each spoon to look like skin and leave the spoons to dry.

2 Creating the three different characters, paint a face on each side of the bowl. Make one happy and one sad.

3 Paint the spoon handles with different colors and let them dry. Then add other "features" – buttons, a collar, spots or stripes. When dry, add a ribbon tie or bow around the neck.

4 Make "hair" from about 10 long strands of wool, string or straw. Tie a shorter piece around the middle to keep them together.

5 When your puppets are ready you can use them to act out the story of *The Runaway Son*. Remember to use both faces of each character as their moods change.